Cara the Cowgirl

'Cara the Cowgirl'
An original concept by Elizabeth Dale
© Elizabeth Dale

Illustrated by Serena Lombardo

Published by MAVERICK ARTS PUBLISHING LTD
Studio 3A, City Business Centre, 6 Brighton Road,
Horsham, West Sussex, RH13 5BB
© Maverick Arts Publishing Limited November 2018
+44 (0)1403 256941

A CIP catalogue record for this book is available at the British Library.

ISBN 978-1-84886-392-7

Maverick
publishing
www.maverickbooks.co.uk

White

This book is rated as: White Band (Guided Reading)

Cara the Cowgirl

By Elizabeth Dale

Illustrated by Serena Lombardo

Chapter 1

Cara is a cowgirl. She loves living in the wild, wild west, where the cacti are as prickly as hedgehogs and the sun is hotter than fried cackleberries.*

She loves her family and friends, but best of all she loves Hop-along, her pony. He's the best friend a cowgirl could have.

Cara is the best cowgirl in Creektown. Well... she's the only cowgirl in Creektown.

*Cackleberries is a cowboy name for eggs.

She spends all day riding Hop-along and rounding up the cows – whether they need rounding up or not!

The people in Creektown aren't used to girls doing cowgirl-type stuff. The other girls love to knit and read books and cook.

Cara likes to do all those things while riding Hop-along. Sometimes she even cooks while she's standing on him. The mid-day sun is so hot that she can easily cook a fried cackleberry!

Everyone can hear Cara coming, because she loves shouting, **"Yee-haw!"**

But she's still learning to throw a lasso. Well, she knows how to throw it, but somehow it always misses its target.

"You're only ten," Cara's dad tells her. "If you keep on practising, I'm sure you'll get better at lassoing soon."

So Cara keeps on trying and trying...

Chapter 2

Finally it's the day of the big round-up. This is the day when the best cows are taken off to market. It's the most exciting day of the year. All the men in Creektown come to Cara's ranch to help. There are cowboys, store-keepers and even the sheriff.

"Can I come to market, too?" Cara begs her dad. "Please! You need all the help you can get."

"But we need your help on the ranch," says Dad. "We'll be gone a long time... and you mustn't miss your lessons."

Cara frowns. She thinks she would learn more useful things by riding to market. She might learn how to catch coyotes and keep other animals away.

She might even find out how to suck the poison out of a deadly snake-bite!

"It's safest if you stay here, Cara," says the sheriff. "We might be attacked by nasty thieves trying to steal our cows. Did you hear that Black Jake just broke out of jail? He's the wickedest, wildest bandit in the west."

All the cowboys look afraid. They'd all heard the awful news. They're terrified of Black Jake.

"Y-you d-d-d-don't want to meet him on the ride to market," stammers one, and the others agree.

"Are you brave, Cara?" asks the sheriff.

Cara hopes he will say she can go with them. So she says. "**Yee-haw,** I am! I'm incredibly, amazingly, wonderfully brave!"

"In that case you're just the person," says the sheriff, and Cara smiles.

But then he hands her his badge and says, "You can be the sheriff while I'm away. I need someone brave to protect the townsfolk for me."

Cara trembles. She isn't that brave! But the town needs her. And at least she will have Hop-along by her side...

She pats her trusty pony. But for some reason he seems a little trembly, too.

At least Cara is allowed to join in the fun of rounding up all the cows.

"Right!" yells her dad when they're finished. "Off to market. Yee-haw!"

"Yee-haw!" shout all the cowboys.

"Yee-haw," whispers Cara as she sadly watches the cowboys galloping off with the cows.

Wiping a tear from her eye, Cara goes to check the hens. Then she feeds the calves and gives Hop-along his tea. Then she fries a quick cackleberry in the heat of the sun, which she eats with a heap of beans.

Finally, it's time to go to town. Cara needs to protect the people of Creektown.

"Giddy-up, Hop-along!" she cries, and they head off together.

Chapter 3

As they ride through Creektown, both Cara and Hop-along are pleased to see that it's very quiet.

There's no one robbing the bank or even stealing sweeties from the store.

Cara smiles bravely as the sun glints on her sheriff's badge. Maybe being sheriff won't be too hard, after all?

"Whoa, boy!" Cara cries, as Hop-along reaches the store.

She jumps off and throws her lasso at the hitching rail. She misses it, but nearly catches a stray cat called Scratchy by mistake.

Cara tries once more to loop the rail. She misses again, but this time she does get Scratchy.

Cara's not very pleased. Neither is Scratchy!

"Oh dear! Lassoing is very hard!" thinks Cara, as she quickly frees the angry cat.

Suddenly a horse comes galloping up Main Street. Cara can see that it's ridden by a very scared farmer. The farmer is wildly waving his hat.

"Look out! Black Jake is coming!" the man yells.
"He knows the sheriff's away. He says he's
going to rob the bank!"

Everyone in the town rushes to hide – behind
chairs, inside wardrobes and under beds.

Suddenly Cara doesn't feel brave any more. She'd love to hide too, but she knows a sheriff has to do what a sheriff has to do. Even a sheriff who's only ten years-old.

Somehow she has to stop Black Jake robbing the bank.

Chapter 4

Cara nervously licks her lips and waits.

Suddenly she hears a horse galloping madly. It must be Igor, Black Jake's horse!

As the horse turns the corner, she sees Black Jake, too.

He hollers, **"Yee-haw!"** as he rides towards her.

Quickly Cara steps into the street. Hop-along snorts loudly, warning her to take care. But as Black Jake gets nearer and nearer, Cara stands tall.

"Stop!" she cries, flinging her arms wide.

But Black Jake doesn't even slow down.

Instead, he heads to one side to pass her. So Cara jumps sideways to block him.

He heads to the other side. So does she.

Hop-along can't bear to watch. He snorts again to warn Cara, then tosses his head... and gallops away.

Cara can't believe it!

Hop-along would never leave her in danger all on her own! Is he going to fetch help? If so, he needs to wait for her!

She spins around and throws her lasso at Hop-along.

Cara's lasso flies up into the air. She watches as it whirls round and round...

...and misses Hop-along completely.

Instead, somehow the lasso falls over Black Jake as he gallops past!

Yee-haw!

Cara can't believe it! She's caught him!

The lasso tightens around Black Jake, and Cara holds tight. But as Igor gallops on, suddenly Cara feels herself being pulled along behind him.

There's no way Cara's letting Black Jake get away. So she keeps hold of the lasso and **whoosh!**

Suddenly she's running along behind Black Jake and Igor.

Chapter 5

As they see poor Cara whizzing past, the people of Creektown are frozen with fear.

Igor races towards Hop-along, who has stopped, horrified, when he sees what's happened to poor Cara. He has to help her!

The brave pony charges towards Igor and then rears up, neighing wildly. Igor is startled – and Black Jake falls off!

Cara slides to a halt. She grins at Black Jake, who's tied up at her feet. She's got him!

Black Jake is furious. "Set me free!" he yells, as he tries to get up – and falls over.

"No way!'" cries Cara.

Somehow the nasty bandit doesn't look nearly so scary with his arms tied to his sides.

"Well done, Hop-along!" she yells. "Let's lock him up!"

The trusty pony grabs the lasso rope in his teeth and together he and Cara pull the angry crook towards the jail. Once inside, Hop-along nudges him into a cell and Cara quickly locks the door behind him.

Black Jake glares at her through the bars.

"Captured by a girl!" he spits. "I'll never live it down. My days of being the wickedest, wildest bandit in the west are over!"

"Hooray!" cheer all the people, rushing in. "Well done, Cara and Hop-along!"

And when the cowboys and sheriff return from the cattle market, they cheer, too.

"You saved the bank!" they cry. "You've jailed Black Jake. Well done, Cara. You're a hero."

"I couldn't have done it without Hop-along!" she replies. "He's a hero, too."

And so they all have a big party with cackleberries and son-of-a-gun stew*. There's also a huge bale of hay for Hop-along.

And at the end of it all, there's only one thing to say –

"Yee-haw!"

The End

*'Son-of-a-gun stew' is a cowboy's name for a stew with anything and everything thrown in!

Book Bands for Guided Reading

The Institute of Education book banding system is a scale of colours that reflects the various levels of reading difficulty. The bands are assigned by taking into account the content, the language style, the layout and phonics. Word, phrase and sentence level work is also taken into consideration.

Maverick Early Readers are a bright, attractive range of books covering the pink to white bands. All of these books have been book banded for guided reading to the industry standard and edited by a leading educational consultant.

Pink
Red
Yellow
Blue
Green
Orange
Turquoise
Purple
Gold
White

To view the whole Maverick Readers scheme, visit our website at
www.maverickearlyreaders.com

Or scan the QR code above to view our scheme instantly!